CORNELIA FUNKE

Illustrated by Kerstin Meyer

A Princess,

A Pirate, AND

ONE WILD BROTHER

Chicken House

SCHOLASTIC INC./NEW YORK

The Princess Knight
Text copyright © 2001 by Cornelia Funke
Illustrations copyright © 2001 by Kerstin Meyer
English translation copyright © 2003 by Anthea Bell

Pirate Girl
Text copyright © 2003 by Cornelia Funke
Illustrations copyright © 2003 by Kerstin Meyer
English translation copyright © 2005 by Chantal Wright

The Wildest Brother
Text copyright © 2004 by Cornelia Funke
Illustrations copyright © 2004 by Kerstin Meyer
English translation copyright © 2006 by Oliver Latsch

All rights reserved. Published by Chicken House, an imprint of Scholastic Inc., *Publishers since 1920*. SCHOLASTIC, CHICKEN HOUSE, and associated logos are trademarks and/or registered trademarks of Scholastic Inc.

ISBN-13: 978-0-545-04241-3
ISBN-10: 0-545-04241-0

10 9 8 7 6 5 4 3 2 1   08 09 10 11 12

Printed in Singapore   46
This collection first published April 2008

TABLE OF CONTENTS

The Princess Knight

King Wilfred the Worthy had three sons.
He brought them up just as his father had brought *him* up,
and they were taught all the things *he* had been taught.
He wanted them to be better than his best knights.

They learned riding and jousting, fighting with swords, and good table manners, too.

They learned how to stride around proudly and how to shout *very* loudly.

And (perhaps most important for princes) they learned how to give orders — to their nursemaids, their servants, their dogs, and their horses.

Then Queen Victoria had a
daughter. But the queen died when the
baby was born. So, the little girl was
called Violetta.

No one would dare tell the king *how* to do anything —
especially how to raise his little girl. So he decided to teach
her the same lessons that he had taught his sons . . .

even though she was so small
she could hardly lift a sword at all!

Her brothers teased her and called her names.
"Itsy-Bitsy Little Vi — little girl can't hurt a fly!"

And they would boast that
they were so strong, even
the most spirited horse
would obey them.

Then they'd strike the heads off practice dummies
so hard that the heads would fly right over the
castle walls!

And they would laugh and laugh at their little sister
as she struggled to mount a horse in her heavy armor,
as if it were the funniest thing they'd ever seen.

"Oh, Emma," said Violetta to her nursemaid one evening, while Emma soothed the little girl's bruises. "I'll never be as strong as my brothers."

"Not as strong, maybe, but you are three times as clever," said Emma sensibly. "Why not ask your father to stop teaching you all this silly fighting and to let you learn something else instead? Embroidery perhaps. Or weaving. Or playing the flute. Something *useful*?"

But Violetta shook her head.

"No, no, no," she said. "That would only make my brothers laugh louder."

So Emma said no more. For she knew the princess was more determined than all the three princes put together.

From that night on, Violetta slipped out of the castle in secret, while the rose gardener's son kept watch for her.

She started to practice all the things her brothers could already do so much better.

Violetta practiced in her own way, without shouting and without using her spurs.

Indeed, she was very quiet about it — as quiet as the night itself.

So, while her brothers grew as tall and strong as King Wilfred's knights, Violetta, who stayed quite small, got better at fighting and riding every day. And her father's horses loved to carry her on their backs.

Violetta became so nimble and quick that when her three
brothers practiced jousting with her, their spears and swords
just hit the empty air. And the princes soon stopped
laughing at her. And they stopped calling her
"Itsy-Bitsy Little Vi!"

Then came the day before Violetta's sixteenth birthday, and the king asked to see her.

"Violetta," said King Wilfred, "I'm going to hold a jousting tournament in honor of your birthday. The victory prize will bring the bravest knights in the land flocking to the castle."

"What will that prize be, Father?" asked Violetta, wondering which horse she would ride, which of her suits of armor would be lightest, and which plume she would wear in her helmet.

"The prize," said King Wilfred, "will be your hand
in marriage. So put on your finest gown
and practice your prettiest smile."

Violetta turned as red as the roses beside the castle moat.

"What!" she cried. "You want *me* to marry some dimwit in a tin suit? Just look at your own knights! They whip their horses and they can't even write their own names!"

Her father was so angry that he locked Violetta up in the castle tower all by herself. Not until the moon was shining high in the sky did the King tell Violetta's youngest brother to let her out.

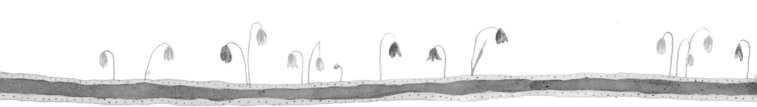

"Stop crying, little sister!" said Violetta's brother. "I'll make sure to win the tournament myself. You certainly can't marry *me*!"

But Violetta shook her head and wiped her eyes on the hem of her dress.

"Thank you," she said, "but I think I'd better just see to it myself."

The next day the field behind the castle was crowded
with knights who had come to fight in the tournament.
King Wilfred sat down to watch. Little did he know that
it wasn't Violetta who sat beside him. It was her nursemaid,
Emma. She wore Violetta's best dress and a veil over her face.

The real Violetta had put on her blackest armor and
saddled her favorite horse. She rode into the arena with
the other knights and gave her title as Sir No-Name.

Trumpets sounded and the tournament to win the
princess's hand began. Knight after knight rode into the
arena — Sigurd the Strong, Harold the Hardy, Percy the
Pitiless — but Sir No-Name defeated them all. He even
knocked the king's sons off their horses and into the dust.

By the end there was no one left who was willing to fight. And Sir No-Name rode over to the king to receive the victory prize.

"Where do you come from, Sir No-Name?" asked the king. "You have brought honor to your family, and my daughter should think herself lucky to take your hand in marriage."

"Oh, I don't think so!" Sir No-Name replied, raising his helmet . . .

"Hello, Father," said Violetta. "What's the prize for a
Princess Knight?"

And for the first time in his life,
her father, the king, was speechless.

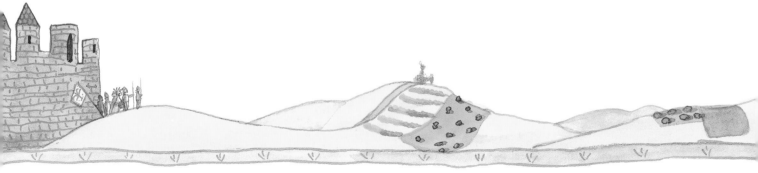

Violetta turned to the defeated knights, sitting battered
and bruised on their horses.

"Very well," she said. "I shall choose my own prize."

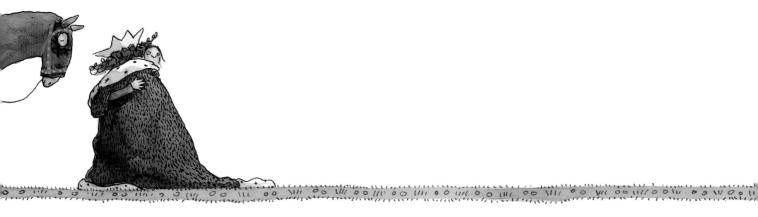

"I hereby proclaim that no one will ever win Princess Violetta's hand in marriage without first defeating Sir No-Name."

Then she turned on her horse and rode away — far, far away. And she didn't return for a year and a day.

And when she did? Why, her father, King Wilfred the Worthy, gave her a horse as black as her armor. And nobody, not even her brothers, challenged the princess ever again.

And who *did* she marry? Well, if you must know, many years later, she married the rose gardener's son and lived happily ever after.

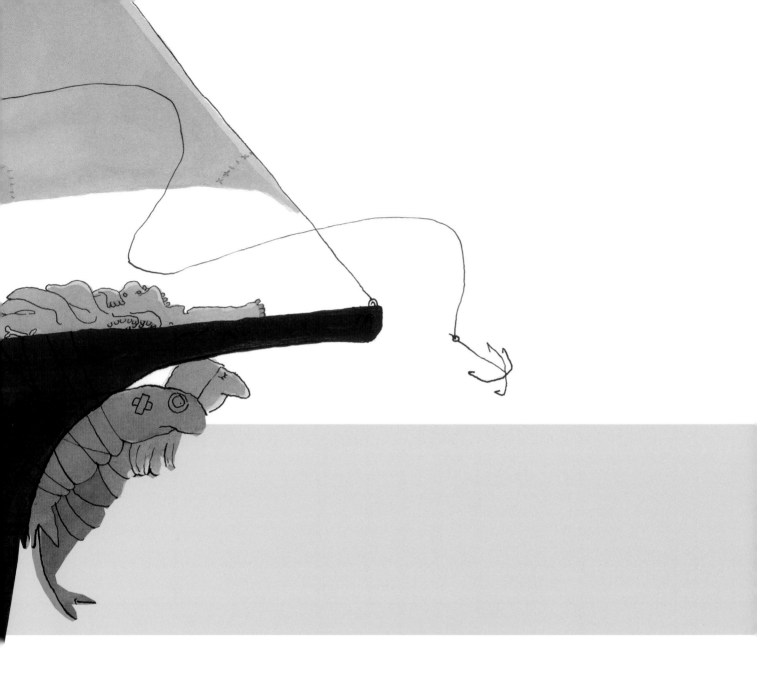

Captain Firebeard was the terror of the high seas. His ship, the *Horrible Haddock*, sailed faster than the wind over the waves. Whenever the *Horrible Haddock* appeared on the horizon, the knees of honest seafaring folk would shake like jelly.

Captain Firebeard had a fearsome crew. His helmsman was Morgan O'Meany. His cook was Cutlass Tom. Bill the Bald, Willy Wooden Hand, Crooked Carl, and twenty more terrible pirates just like them made up the rest of the motley bunch.

When Firebeard's crew boarded a ship, nothing was safe. They stole the silver spoons and the captain's uniform. They stole the ship's figurehead, the pots and pans, the hammocks, and the sails. And, of course, they stole ALL the casks of rum.

But one day Firebeard robbed a ship that he really should have left alone. On board was a little girl named Molly.

Molly was off on a trip to see her grandma.

The pirates leaped on board with an earsplitting roar. Molly tried hiding among the ropes, but Morgan O'Meany soon fished her out.

"What shall we do with her?" he said with a smirk.

"Take her with us, you fool!" bellowed Firebeard. "Her parents will pay a handsome ransom for such a little treasure. And if not, then we'll feed her to the sharks."

"You'll be sorry for this!" cried Molly.

But Morgan O'Meany rolled her up like a herring and tossed her on board the *Horrible Haddock.*

When the sun had gone down, Bill the Bald dragged
Molly to see the captain.

"All right, tell me your parents' names and address,
or else!" growled Captain Firebeard.

"Will not!" Molly growled back. "If I told you my
mother's name, you'd be so scared, you'd cry like a baby!"
At this, all the pirates howled with laughter.

So Molly was put to work. She peeled potatoes and cleaned boots. She polished cutlasses, patched sails, and scrubbed the deck. Soon every bone in her body ached.

Three times a day Firebeard asked her, "Name and address?"

But Molly just smiled.

"Feed her to the sharks!" roared Willy Wooden Hand.

But Firebeard ground his teeth and said, "She'll talk before long."

Every night the pirates had a party. They drank rum, staggered across the deck, danced on the ship's rigging, and bawled out the rudest songs.

But Molly had a plan. While the pirates were carousing, she wrote secret messages and popped them into empty bottles. When the pirates were safely snoring in their bunks, she tossed the bottles into the sea. Molly did this every night.

One night the pirates partied until
dawn. But this time, they fell asleep
on the deck.

Molly tiptoed over the tangle of arms and
legs and threw her bottle over the ship's rail.
Splish! Splash! It landed in the deep, wide sea.

"Hey! What was that?" yelled Morgan O'Meany. The pirates staggered over to the rail.

"It's a message in a bottle!" they all cried.

"Bring it to me!" shouted Captain Firebeard. "Now!"

The pirates dived to the bottom of the sea. They searched and searched, but Molly's message had bobbed away. Soaking wet, they crawled back on deck, cursing.

"Tell me what you wrote!" demanded Captain Firebeard.

But Molly just kicked at his wooden leg.

Firebeard turned as red as a lobster. "NOW it's time to feed her to the sharks!" he roared.

But a cry from above stopped him.

"P . . . P . . . P . . . Pirates!"

shouted Ten-Pint Ted from the crow's nest.

"Nonsense!" scoffed Firebeard. "*We're* the only pirates around here."

But he was wrong. A ship with red sails was
speeding toward them. A giant black flag with a skull
and crossbones fluttered from its mast.
"Who in the name of Neptune's beard
is that?" stuttered Firebeard.

"That's my mom!" Molly grinned.

"It's Barbarous Bertha herself!" wailed the crew of the *Horrible Haddock.*

Firebeard turned as white as a sheet and his pirates rolled their eyes in fear. This time it was *their* knees that were shaking.

And Bill the Bald's false teeth almost flew out of his mouth.

The ship with the red sails drew closer and closer.
Barbarous Bertha stood at the prow, swinging her cutlass.
"Wait until she sees my hands!" said Molly.
"They're red and raw from peeling potatoes. That will
make my mom maddest of all!"
Firebeard and his pirates groaned with terror.

Soon Barbarous Bertha was alongside the *Horrible Haddock*. Her ferocious crew swung themselves over the rail with a terrible roar.

"We're here at last, my pirate girl!" cried Barbarous Bertha, throwing Molly high into the air.

"We got your message. Your grandma was beginning to wonder where you were. Now, how nasty can we be to these piratical nincompoops?"

"Well!" said Molly. "That's easy."

From that day on, Captain Firebeard and his pirate crew had no time to think about raiding ships.

Willy Wooden Hand scrubbed the deck.

Morgan O'Meany and Cutlass Tom peeled vegetables from morning until night.

Captain Firebeard polished Barbarous Bertha's boots fourteen times a week.

And Molly was finally able to visit her grandma!

THE WILDEST BROTHER

Some mornings when Ben wakes up
he is a **WILD WOLF**.

Or a knight.

Or a **MONSTER** covered in **SCARS**.

He paints them on his face with Anna's makeup.

He always creeps very quietly into her room.

But sometimes Anna catches him.

Then she gives him a good tickling.
Anna is Ben's big sister.

Big sisters,
unfortunately, know
exactly where
little brothers are
ticklish.

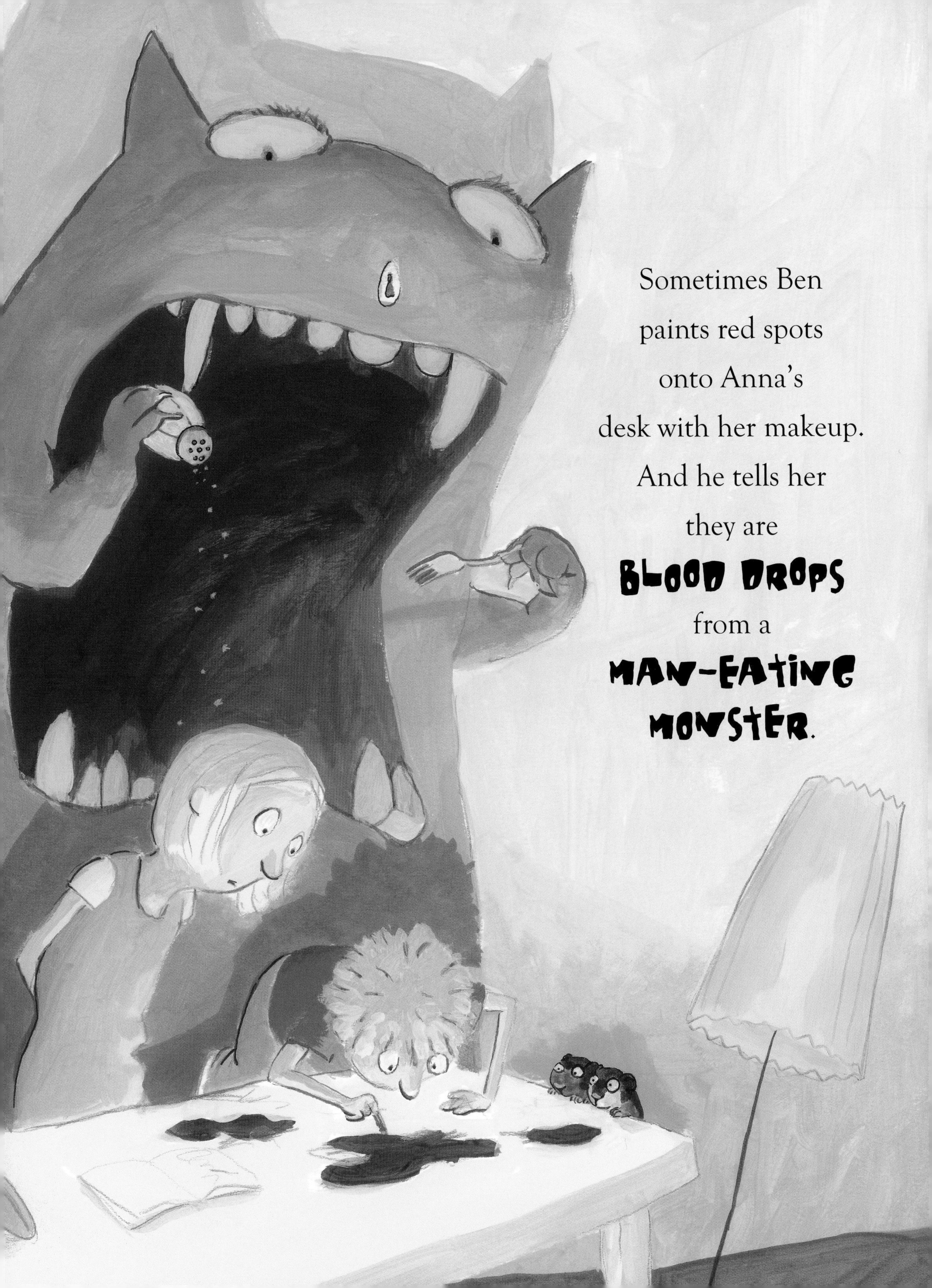

Sometimes Ben
paints red spots
onto Anna's
desk with her makeup.
And he tells her
they are
BLOOD DROPS
from a
**MAN-EATING
MONSTER.**

And that he'll protect her.

After all, he's lionhearted and elephant-strong.

Then Anna has to hide in the wardrobe.

Without giggling.

Because giggling makes monster-hunters terribly angry.

Anna is only allowed to make monster noises.

She's really good at it.

She **GRUNTS** and **SNORTS** and **GROWLS**.

And Ben, lionhearted and
elephant-strong,

fetches his
three plastic swords,
pumpkin-sized water pistol,
and rubber knife,

and fights until his face
turns bright red

and the

MAN-EATING
MONSTER

is as quiet as a mouse.
Then Anna can come out
of the wardrobe again.

But Ben
can't stop to
wipe the
red spots off
Anna's desk.

Because
three
**MOLDY
GREEN
GHOSTS**
are still
HOWLING
in the
bathroom.

And Ben has to tear them to shreds
and flush them down the toilet—right now.

There's also the
SLIME-BURPING MONSTER
who loves to lick out

the pots in the kitchen.

Fearlessly Ben throws him off
the balcony.

Then, using a jump rope, Ben ties up the **BURGLAR** who sneaks into the house once a week.

All this fighting is exhausting! So exhausting that once Ben even knocked one of Anna's horse posters off the wall.

But Ben does protect Anna
from all the **FOXES** and **WOLVES**
in the garden so Anna can
pick dandelion leaves in peace
for the guinea pigs.

Ben can't help Anna pick the leaves, though.
He has to keep an eye on the **BEARS** lurking
behind the bushes. They are just waiting
for the chance to **GOBBLE UP** such a tasty big sister.

Yes, Ben really has to fight quite a lot.

All day long, in fact.

His muscles have already grown big from it all.

But in the evening,
when Night
presses her soot-black face
against the window
and the heating creaks
like the sound of a thousand biting beetles,
Ben crawls into Anna's bed.
Then she protects him—
from Night's soot-black face
and the biting beetles.

And it is *sooo* wonderful

to have a big, strong sister.

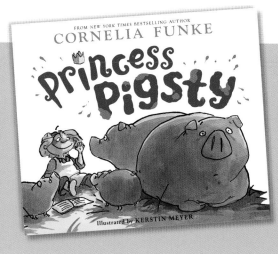

What would YOU do if Santa landed in your neighborhood?

"The story is magical . . ." —*The Washington Post*

0-439-78204-X $15.99 US/$19.99 CAN

A new twist on a knight's tale!

When her magician parents mistakenly turn themselves into pigs, it's up to Igraine to face her fears and save the family castle.

0-439-90379-3 $16.99 US/$19.99 CAN

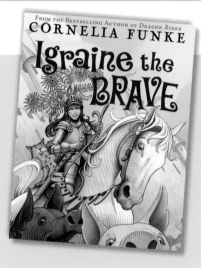

There is a mythical place where dragons can live in peace forever...

"Marvelous stuff for dreaming adventurers of any age." —Clive Barker

0-439-45695-9 $14.99 US/$18.99

Visit www.CorneliaFunkeFans.com